P9-BBU-353

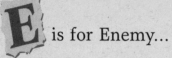 is for Enemy...

The kids peered over the hedge. A man and a woman got out of the car. The man was short and was wearing a green suit and a purple tie.

"That's him!" Josh whispered. "The guy who was following us before!"

The kids watched the man and the woman talk for a few minutes, then get back into the car. But they didn't drive away.

"What the heck are they doing?" Josh asked.

Dink gulped. He put his hand over the envelope hidden under his shirt.

"They're waiting for me," he said.

A to Z Mysteries™

The Empty Envelope

The A to Z Mysteries™ series!

The Absent Author

The Bald Bandit

The Canary Caper

The Deadly Dungeon

The Empty Envelope

A to Z Mysteries™

The Empty Envelope

by Ron Roy

illustrated by
John Steven Gurney

A STEPPING STONE BOOK™

Random House · New York

JOHN-PAUL

Text copyright © 1998 by Ron Roy.
Illustrations copyright © 1998 by John Steven Gurney.
All rights reserved under International and Pan-American Copyright Conventions.
Published in the United States by Random House, Inc., New York, and simultaneously
in Canada by Random House of Canada Limited, Toronto.

www.randomhouse.com/kids/

Library of Congress Cataloging-in-Publication Data
Roy, Ron. The empty envelope / by Ron Roy ; illustrated by John Steven Gurney.
p. cm. — (A to Z mysteries)   "A Stepping Stone book."
SUMMARY: Dink and his friends unearth the mysterious truth behind the envelopes
incorrectly delivered to his house.
ISBN 0-679-89054-8 (trade). — ISBN 0-679-99054-2 (lib. bdg.)
[1. Mystery and detective stories.] I. Gurney, John, ill. II. Title.
III. Series: Roy, Ron. A to Z mysteries.
PZ7.R8139Em 1998 97-31711   [Fic] — dc21

Printed in the United States of America 30 29

A STEPPING STONE BOOK is a trademark of Random House, Inc.

A TO Z MYSTERIES is a trademark of Random House, Inc.

This one is for Jim Thomas
−R.R.

To my neighbor, Jake
−J.S.G.

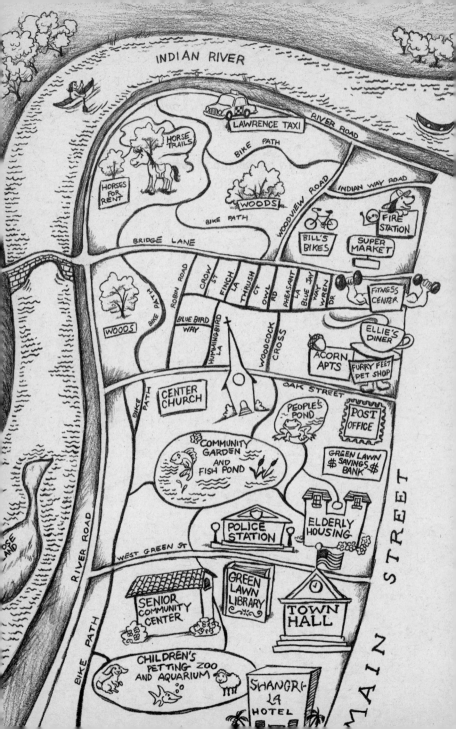

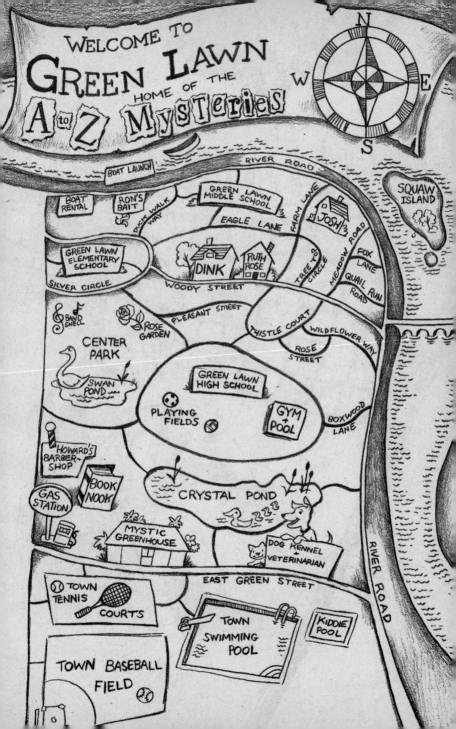

Chapter 1

"I got it! I got it!" Josh yelled as he raced across Dink's backyard. He leaped into the air, missed the volleyball, and fell in a heap.

Dink laughed. "You got it, all right!"

"Way to go, Natie!" Ruth Rose cried. She gave her four-year-old brother, Nate, a high five. "You just scored us another point!"

Nate blushed and smiled shyly at his big sister.

Josh got up and grinned. "Okay, I'm through foolin' around! From now on, Josh and Dink will rule!"

Just then they heard a beep. "It's Ruby with the mail," Ruth Rose said.

Josh dropped the volleyball. "I wonder if you'll get another blue envelope," he said to Dink. "I can't wait to read what Mother has to say today!"

Dink ran to the front just as Ruby waved from her truck and drove away. He opened the mailbox and reached in.

He pulled out two bills for his parents and a letter in a blue envelope for him.

In the past week, Dink had received four other letters in blue envelopes. This was the fifth. Each envelope was addressed to D. Duncan, Green Lawn, CO 06040. But the notes inside were to someone named Doris—from her mother!

Dink returned to his backyard. He held the letter up. "Another one," he said.

"Well, open it," Josh said.

Dink ripped open the envelope and felt inside for the note.

"There's nothing in here," he said. "It's empty."

Ruth Rose peered into the envelope. "Why would Mother send an empty envelope?" she asked.

Dink shrugged. "Let's go in the house. I want to check out the other letters again."

The kids trooped into Dink's kitchen. A covered plate sat on the counter.

"My mom made us some sandwiches," Dink said.

Nate reached for the plate, but his sister stopped him. "Look at those hands! Let's wash up at the sink, Nate."

Dink pulled the other four envelopes from a drawer and laid them on the table side by side. They all looked the same.

"Can I get some juice?" Josh opened the fridge before Dink could answer.

Dink just nodded as he sat and stared at the envelopes. The return address on each was O. Bird, 10 Carroll St., Brooklyn, NY 11234. "I don't know anyone in Brooklyn," he said, "let alone someone named O. Bird."

Dink dropped his eyes to the middle of one of the envelopes. "Hey, look at this!" he said suddenly. He pointed to the CO in his address. "Isn't CO the

O. BIRD
10 CARROLL ST
BROOKLYN, NY 11234

D. DUNCAN
GREEN LAWN, CO.
0 6 0 4 0

abbreviation for Colorado?"

Josh and Ruth Rose each grabbed an envelope.

"Yeah, you're right," Josh said. "Connecticut is CT, not CO."

Dink looked at his friends. "The zip code is right, but the state is wrong!"

"Or maybe it's the state that's right and the zip code that's wrong," Ruth Rose suggested.

"What do you mean?" Josh asked.

"Maybe these letters were supposed to go to some D. Duncan in Green Lawn, Colorado," Ruth Rose said. "Whoever O. Bird is just wrote down the wrong zip code."

"I know how to find out," Dink said.

He walked over to the phone and dialed information. He asked the long-distance operator for O. Bird's number.

"There isn't?" he said. "Okay, thanks anyway." Dink hung up. "There's no

O. Bird listed in Brooklyn."

"Well," Josh said, grabbing a sand-wich, "you're the only D. Duncan in Green Lawn."

"In Green Lawn, *Connecticut*," Dink said.

Josh sighed. "Anyway, let's eat."

They wolfed down the peanut butter

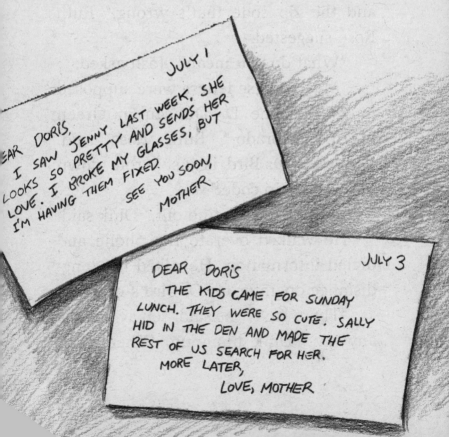

JULY 1

EAR DORIS,
I SAW JENNY LAST WEEK. SHE LOOKS SO PRETTY AND SENDS HER LOVE. I BROKE MY GLASSES, BUT I'M HAVING THEM FIXED.
SEE YOU SOON,
MOTHER

JULY 3

DEAR DORIS
THE KIDS CAME FOR SUNDAY LUNCH. THEY WERE SO CUTE. SALLY HID IN THE DEN AND MADE THE REST OF US SEARCH FOR HER.
MORE LATER,
LOVE, MOTHER

and grape jam sandwiches.

"Read the notes again, Dink," Ruth Rose said after a few minutes. "Maybe there's a clue about who they're really meant for."

Dink opened the envelopes, pulled out the four notes, and laid them side by side.

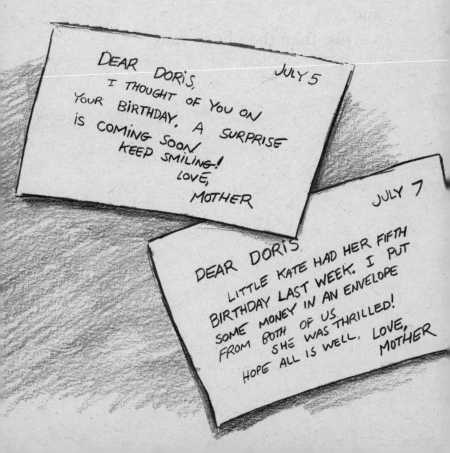

DEAR DORIS,   JULY 5
I THOUGHT OF YOU ON
YOUR BIRTHDAY. A SURPRISE
IS COMING SOON!
KEEP SMILING!
LOVE,
MOTHER

JULY 7
DEAR DORIS,
LITTLE KATE HAD HER FIFTH
BIRTHDAY LAST WEEK. I PUT
SOME MONEY IN AN ENVELOPE
FROM BOTH OF US.
SHE WAS THRILLED!
HOPE ALL IS WELL. LOVE,
MOTHER

Josh picked up the fifth envelope. He turned it upside down and shook it. "Maybe someone stole the last letter," he whispered. He made mysterious eyes at Dink.

"Maybe spies are watching your mail," he said in a creepy voice. "Maybe they're alien kidnappers from Neptune and..."

Just then the phone rang.

Chapter 2

Dink answered the phone.

"Is this D. Duncan?" a woman's voice asked.

"I'm Donald Duncan," Dink said. "But my friends call me Dink."

"Well, Dink," the voice said, "I'm Doris Duncan from Colorado. I think you may have some letters that belong to me."

Dink covered the phone and turned to Josh and Ruth Rose. "It's some woman from Colorado asking for the letters!" he whispered excitedly.

"Hello? Are you still there?" the woman asked. "Don't hang up!"

Dink spoke into the phone again. "Um...I got five blue envelopes this week."

"Well, those letters are mine. They're very important," Doris Duncan said. "When can I get them back?"

Dink glanced across the kitchen. "They're right here on the table," he told Doris Duncan. "Do you want me to send them to you?"

"No!" the woman snapped. "Don't send them anywhere! I'm at the Shangri-la Hotel right now. How do I find you?"

"Well, I guess you could come to my house," Dink said. He gave her directions to 22 Woody Street and hung up.

"What was that all about?" Ruth Rose asked.

Dink sat at the table again. "That was Doris Duncan. The letters are hers, and she's coming right over to get them."

"From Colorado?" Josh said.

"No, she's at the Shangri-la. She should be here in a few minutes."

"She's in Connecticut?" Ruth Rose said. "That's weird."

Dink nodded. "Yeah, and another thing. She sounded mad, like I took the letters on purpose."

"This is so lame," Josh said, yawning. "You got the letters by mistake, and some woman is coming over to get them." He stood up and stretched. "Let's go finish the game."

Dink slipped the notes back inside their envelopes, then stood them between the salt and pepper shakers.

Ruth Rose poked the envelopes. "Don't you guys think it's weird that she came all the way to Connecticut just for some notes from her mom?"

"Maybe Dink can ask her when she gets here," Josh said. "Now can we *please* play volleyball?"

Ruth Rose stood up. "What could be so important about these letters?" she wondered out loud.

Ten minutes later, Dink heard someone calling, "You there, young man!"

Dink ran to the side yard and saw a tall woman walking up his sidewalk. He jogged out front to meet her.

"Hi. Are you Mrs. Duncan?"

The woman towered over Dink. "I'm Ms. Duncan. Are you Dink?"

Dink had to bend his head backward to see the tall woman's face. She had black hair and dark, squinty eyes. She was clutching a purse in her large, strong-looking hand.

"Well, are you the boy I talked to or not?" the woman demanded.

Dink gulped. "Yes, ma'am. I'll get the letters," he said.

"Thank you," the woman said. Suddenly she sounded almost nice. "They're from my mother, Bessie Duncan. She died last month. These were her last letters to me."

Dink went inside to the kitchen. He walked over to the table to get the letters. But they were gone!

Dink looked around the kitchen. The letters weren't on the counter, the fridge, or the stove.

Dink looked on the floor under the table. He saw a few crumbs from lunch, but no blue envelopes.

"What's the matter?" Ruth Rose said. She and Josh were peering through the back screen door.

"I can't find the letters!" Dink told

his friends. "Didn't I leave them on the table after we ate lunch?"

Ruth Rose pushed open the door and came in. "I think so."

She looked behind the toaster, the coffee maker, and the microwave.

"Help us look, Josh," Dink said. "That lady is waiting! The letters are from her mom, and she died last month!"

Josh stepped inside, and the kids searched the kitchen. The letters had vanished.

"Guess I'd better go tell her," Dink muttered, shaking his head. "I *know* I left them on the table!"

He walked through the living room and opened the front door. Doris Duncan was standing where he'd left her.

Dink swallowed. "I...um, I'm real sorry, but I can't find the letters."

The woman glared down at him. "What do you mean?" she said. "When I called, you said you had them. Where are they?"

Dink felt his face turn red. "I don't know," he mumbled. "They were on the kitchen table, and now they're not. My friends even helped me look."

The woman stared over Dink's shoulder. She looked as if she wanted to barge past him and search the house herself.

"I'll ask my mom to help when she gets home," Dink said. "Can you come back later?"

Doris Duncan tapped her fingers on her purse. "I'll be back at six o'clock sharp," she said. "I'll expect my letters then, young man!"

"Don't worry, we'll find them," Dink assured her. "My mom can find anything. She's a real neat Nelly!"

The woman sniffed, then stomped down the sidewalk toward the street.

Dink watched her go, then turned around and bumped into Josh.

"I'm telling your mom you called her a neat Nelly," Josh said, grinning.

"It's not polite to listen to people's conversations, Joshua," Dink said. He headed back to the kitchen.

"Guys, look at this," Ruth Rose said. She was pointing at a small purple hand print on the kitchen table. "I thought I wiped the table."

Josh bent over and sniffed the purple print. "It's grape jam."

Ruth Rose grinned. "I think I know who took the envelopes," she said.

Chapter 3

The kids marched next door to Ruth Rose's house. They found Nate in the living room watching a video. His fingers and mouth were stained purple.

"Natie, did you take Dink's letters?" Ruth Rose asked.

Nate looked at his sister with big blue eyes. He shook his head. "Nope."

Ruth Rose glanced at Dink and Josh. She rolled her eyes. "Okay, then who took them? We found your jammy fingerprints."

Nate hid his hands under his T-shirt. "Steggy did," he said softly.

Dink knelt down next to Nate. "Where did Steggy put the envelopes?" he asked.

Nate shrugged, watching two dancing dinosaurs on TV.

"Who the heck is Steggy?" Josh asked.

"His favorite dinosaur," Ruth Rose said. She turned off the TV. "Natie, Dink really needs his letters. Can you show us where Steggy put them?"

Nate let out a big sigh. He got up and walked into the kitchen. The kids followed.

Nate pulled open the refrigerator door. A stuffed stegosaur sat on a shelf next to a bowl of strawberry Jell-O.

Steggy had five blue envelopes in his mouth.

Josh laughed. "Yo, Nate, don't you know dinosaurs hate the cold?"

Nate pulled Steggy off the shelf and shut the door. "Steggy's playing mailman. It's hot outside," he said.

Ruth Rose handed the envelopes to Dink. "It's not nice to take things without asking," she told her brother.

"It's okay, Natie," Dink said, examining the envelopes for purple smudges. He wanted the letters to look perfect for Doris Duncan.

Dink found a few splotches of grape jam and wiped them off on his pants. When he looked for more purple stains, he noticed the return address again.

"This is weird," he said.

Dink showed the return address to Josh and Ruth Rose. "Doris Duncan's mother's name is Bessie Duncan. So why are the letters from O. Bird?"

"Maybe O. Bird mailed the notes for her after she died," Josh said.

Dink laid the envelopes in a row on the kitchen table. He pulled out the notes and placed them next to their envelopes.

"But what about this?" Dink said.

"The letters are all dated last week. But Doris Duncan told me her mom died last *month!*"

"Mind if I get us all some milk?" Josh asked.

"Go ahead," Ruth Rose said, picking up the empty envelope. "And why would anyone send her own daughter an envelope with nothing in it?"

Dink nodded. "It doesn't make any sense," he said, "unless these letters aren't really from her mother."

"But why would Doris tell us a story like that?" Ruth Rose wondered.

Josh picked up one of the letters. He read it quickly. Then he carefully spilled a small puddle of milk on the writing.

"What're you doing!" Dink yelled. "Doris Duncan will kill me!"

"Wait a sec." Josh smeared the milk around with his finger. "I read in a spy comic that if you pour milk on invisible ink, you can read it," he said. "Maybe there's a secret message!"

They all hunched over the letter. No hidden writing appeared. But now there was a wet, milky blotch over some of the words.

"Thanks a lot, Josh," Dink said. "Wait till Doris Duncan sees this!"

Ruth Rose blotted the letter with a paper napkin. "Don't worry, it'll dry," she said. She waved the letter in the air, then held it up to the sunny window.

"It'd better," Dink said, giving Josh an "or you'll be sorry!" look.

"Guys, look at this!" Ruth Rose said. "There are two pinholes in the paper. The holes go right through the letters H and D!"

Josh grabbed another letter. He held it next to Ruth Rose's at the window. "This one has a hole too!" he said.

"There's a tiny one right through the letter J!"

Dink jumped up and looked at the pinholes. Then he stared at his friends. "Maybe there really *is* a secret message!" he said.

Chapter 4

The kids examined the other two notes. They found pinholes through the letters O, F, and E.

"H, D, J, O, F, and E all have holes through them," Dink said, writing the letters on a pad.

"Maybe the letters spell a secret message," Ruth Rose said. "Let's try to make words out of them." She grabbed the pad.

"I get *hoe, Joe, doe, foe,* and *fed,*" she said after a minute.

"How about *of, Ed, oh,* and *he,*" Dink suggested.

"Those words don't make any sense," Josh said. "Maybe each letter stands for a word. You know, like SCUBA."

Dink and Ruth Rose just stared at him.

"You know, SCUBA? S, C, U, B, and A? The letters stand for 'self-contained underwater breathing apparatus.'"

Dink grinned. "Josh, how come you look so dumb, but you're really so smart?"

Josh grinned right back. "How come *you* look so dumb, and you really are?"

"Guys, stop fooling around," Ruth Rose said. "Let's figure out what these letters mean."

The kids spent ten minutes trying to

make a message out of the letters J, H, D, O, F, and E.

"I give up," Dink said finally.

"Wait a minute," Josh said. "Maybe Mother's already shown us the secret words." He picked up one of the notes and peered at the pinholes. "Look," he said. "This hole is in the first E in *envelope*. Maybe it's the word *envelope* that's part of the code!"

Dink and Ruth Rose arranged the four notes by date. Then they looked at the words next to the pinholes.

Dink wrote down six words: *Jenny, hid, den, on, fifth, envelope.*

Ruth Rose started to read them out loud, then suddenly grinned. "Listen, guys. *'Jenny hidden on fifth envelope.'*"

"Awesome!" Josh said, giving Ruth Rose a big grin.

"The one that came today is the fifth envelope," Dink said, holding it up. "But who—or what—is Jenny?"

"The message says Jenny is *on* the envelope," Josh said. "But all I see are the stamps."

"Don't forget the ink and glue," Dink said.

"What about looking for the letters J, E, N, N, and Y in the addresses?" Ruth Rose suggested.

"E, N, N, and Y are there," Josh said

after a minute. "But there's no J."

"That leaves the stamps," Dink said. The stamps were pictures of big yellow sunflowers. "I don't see any Jenny there."

"Guys, look," Ruth Rose said. She grabbed the other envelopes. "The first four envelopes have just one stamp each. But the one that came today has three."

"You're right," Dink said. "I wonder why." He rubbed his fingers across the three sunflower stamps. "I feel something under there!" he said.

Dink held the envelope up to the window. "There's something dark under those stamps," he said. "I can see an outline!"

Chapter 5

"I'm going to boil some water," Ruth Rose said. "My grandfather used to collect stamps. He showed me how to steam 'em off envelopes."

Ruth Rose ran water into the tea-kettle and set the kettle on the burner. Then she turned on the stove.

The kids sat and stared at it.

"Sure is taking a long time to boil," Dink muttered, brushing his fingertips over the sunflower stamps.

Suddenly steam began whistling out of the kettle spout. Dink handed Ruth Rose the empty envelope.

Ruth Rose held the envelope so the stamps were right over the kettle's spout.

In a few seconds, moisture began gathering on the stamps. Then the stamps began to peel away from the envelope.

"Cool!" Josh said. "I feel like a spy!"

Ruth Rose shut off the stove. Using the tip of a toothpick, she removed the three sunflower stamps from the envelope.

Hidden beneath the stamps, covered with cellophane, was a smaller stamp. It was blue. In the center of the stamp was a picture of an old-fashioned airplane. The plane was flying upside down.

Dink removed the cellophane. "It's an old stamp," he said.

Josh poked a finger at the stamp. "The dumb thing is printed wrong," he muttered. "What's the big deal about an upside-down airplane stamp?"

Ruth Rose studied the stamp. "Maybe it's valuable," she said. "My grandfather has a stamp that's worth two hundred dollars!"

"I wonder if Doris Duncan knew this was here," Dink said.

The kids looked at each other. Then they stared at the little blue stamp.

"We should go to the library and look at a book about stamps," Ruth Rose said finally.

Dink glanced at the kitchen clock. "We better make it fast. Doris Duncan will be back in less than an hour!"

Dink slipped the stamp inside the empty envelope and stuck all five envelopes under his shirt. "Okay, let's go," he said.

Ruth Rose went to the bottom of the hall stairs. "MOM, I'M GOING TO THE LIBRARY!" she yelled.

They hurried through the living

room, out the door, and down Ruth Rose's front sidewalk.

As they started up Woody Street, Josh nudged Dink with his elbow. "Look. There's some weird guy watching us." He pointed at a dark car parked on the other side of the street.

Ruth Rose looked. "What guy?"

They all looked. There was no one in the car.

"Come on," Dink said. "We're running out of time!"

The kids ran all the way to the library. When they charged up the front steps, they were out of breath.

Mrs. Mackleroy looked up as they burst through the door. "Slow down, kids," she said. "Why, your faces are red as beets!"

"Hi, Mrs. Mackleroy," Ruth Rose panted. "Can you show us a book about stamps?"

"What kind of stamps, Ruth Rose? United States? Foreign? We have many, many books about stamps, dear."

"Do you have one about stamps with pictures of upside-down airplanes?" Dink asked.

Mrs. Mackleroy smiled. "You mean *inverts*," she said. "Stamps that were printed upside down by mistake."

She walked to a shelf and returned with a big flat book. "You should find your stamp in here," Mrs. Mackleroy said.

"Thanks a lot," Dink said.

Dink carried the book over to a corner table. He set it down, looked around, then pulled the envelopes from inside his shirt.

He carefully removed the blue stamp and placed it on the table.

"There's a zillion upside-down stamps in here," Josh said, riffling through the pages. "How do we find ours?"

"Try the index," Dink said. "Under Jenny."

Josh turned to the index in the back of the book. He ran his finger down the J section. "No Jenny," he said.

"Try looking under airplanes," Ruth Rose suggested.

"Good idea!" Josh backed up a few pages to the A's. He found a listing for airplanes and turned to page 329.

And there it was. A picture of the little blue stamp.

Below the picture was a drawing of the airplane, only bigger. The caption read: CURTIS JENNY SINGLE-ENGINE AIRPLANE.

"Hey!" Josh said. "Jenny's the airplane!"

Silently the kids read the paragraph about the stamp.

"OH MY GOSH!" Ruth Rose yelled.

Mrs. Mackleroy tapped her pencil on the desk. "Ruth Rose, please," she said.

Dink picked up the little Jenny stamp. His fingers were shaking.

"This is worth *fifty thousand dollars!*" he whispered.

Chapter 6

"F-f-fifty thou...holy moly!" Josh squeaked.

The kids stared at the small blue stamp. After a minute, Dink slipped it back inside the envelope and put it in his pocket.

"No wonder Doris Duncan came all the way to Connecticut!" Ruth Rose said.

Dink nodded. "Yeah. She was after

the stamp the whole time. I knew that story about her mother smelled fishy."

Josh closed the stamp book. "Well, we still have to give the stamp to her."

Dink and Ruth Rose looked at each other.

"Don't we?" Josh asked.

"I guess..." Dink said.

"What do you mean, 'I guess'?" Josh said. "It's hers, Dink. It was on her letter, no matter who sent it to her."

"But why was it hidden?" Dink asked. "Why the whole story about Doris's mother? Why the fake letters? Unless..."

"Unless what?" Josh asked.

Dink looked at Josh and Ruth Rose. "Unless the stamp is stolen..."

"Yes!" Ruth Rose said. "It's worth so much money! Maybe O. Bird stole it. Then he—or she—had to find a way to get it to Doris, so they thought up the letters from 'Mother.'"

Josh just looked at them. "You guys are crazy," he finally said. "Besides, there's no way to be sure."

Ruth Rose jumped up. "O. Bird sent the letters from New York, right? Maybe that's where the stamp was stolen!"

Ruth Rose hurried over to Mrs. Mackleroy's desk, spoke to her quickly, then came back.

"What's going on?" Dink asked.

"Mrs. Mackleroy is getting us the last few weeks' *New York Times*," Ruth Rose said. "We can check to see if there's anything about a missing stamp."

Dink looked at the clock. "Five-fifteen. Doris Duncan will be at my house in forty-five minutes!"

Mrs. Mackleroy walked over and dumped a pile of *New York Times*es on their table. "Here you are, kids. Good luck!"

Josh stared at the mountain of papers. "Geez, it'll take us all night to read these!"

"We don't have all night," Dink said, reaching for the pile. "Start reading!"

The kids each took a stack. They set aside the sections they didn't want, like sports, real estate, and entertainment.

For almost half an hour they turned pages.

The clock above Mrs. Mackleroy's desk ticked the minutes away.

"My eyes are getting blurry," Josh said. "There sure is a lot of stolen stuff in New York! Some guy even stole a chimpanzee from the zoo!"

Dink's back was hurting from bending over the table. His head ached, too, and his fingers were smudged gray from ink.

And then he found it.

"Here it is!" Dink said. He pointed to a headline and read:

SENIOR CITIZEN FINDS, THEN LOSES, FORTUNE

JUNE 20. Miss Clementine Painter, 73, was rich for a short time, but now she's poor again. While emptying her vacuum cleaner, she found a rare stamp among the dust. The stamp, worth more than $50,000, was later stolen from her room. New York City police are investigating.

Josh gulped. "You were right, Dink," he whispered. "You can't give the stamp to Doris Duncan!"

Mrs. Mackleroy approached their table. "I have to close up soon," she said.

Dink whipped his head around to look at the clock. Five-forty-eight! "Guys, we have twelve minutes before Doris Duncan comes back to my house!"

The kids thanked Mrs. Mackleroy, stacked the newspapers, and hurried out of the library.

On the library steps, Dink said, "Maybe we should tell Officer Fallon about Doris Duncan."

"But we still can't prove she did anything wrong," Josh said.

"Josh is right, Dink," Ruth Rose said. "Doris Duncan never got the letters or the stamp. If you tell Officer

Fallon that she and O. Bird stole it, they'll say, 'Prove it!'"

"But what am I gonna do?" Dink asked. "It's almost six o'clock! I have to tell Doris Duncan something!"

The kids began walking toward Woody Street.

"I have an idea!" Ruth Rose said. "Why don't we glue the sunflower stamps back on the empty envelope, then hand over all five letters to Doris Duncan? She'll probably take them to her hotel room to read. Then we can run back here, give the Jenny stamp to Officer Fallon, and tell him the whole story."

"But how does that prove she's guilty?" Dink asked.

"Because then she'll have the letters!" Josh said.

Ruth Rose nodded. "And when Officer Fallon gets the letters from

Doris and reads the hidden message, he'll know she and O. Bird stole the stamp."

Dink grinned. "Right. Then we can show him what we just found in the newspaper. Okay, let's go!"

As they hurried down the library steps, Dink saw a dark car pull away from the curb.

"Hey, Josh, isn't that the same car you saw parked on my street?" he asked.

"Yeah, and the same weird-looking guy is driving!" Josh said.

"Josh, there wasn't anyone in that car," Ruth Rose said.

"Maybe he ducked down when you looked," Josh said. "But I know I saw someone in the driver's seat!"

"Whoever it is, we have to get going," Dink said. "It's nearly six o'clock!"

The kids ran up Main Street.

They took a shortcut through Center Park, then raced past the rose garden.

They were out of breath by the time they reached Woody Street.

A few houses away from Dink's, Josh suddenly grabbed Dink and Ruth Rose. He yanked them down behind Miss Alubicky's front hedge.

"What's wrong?" Dink asked.

"That same car is parked in front of your house again!" Josh said.

The kids peered over the hedge. A man and a woman got out of the car. Dink recognized Doris Duncan. The man was short and dressed in a green suit and purple tie.

"That's him!" Josh whispered. "The guy I saw in the car before!"

The kids watched Doris and the man talk for a few minutes, then get back into the car. But the car didn't drive away.

"What the heck are they doing?" Josh asked.

Dink gulped. He put his hand over the envelope holding the $50,000 stamp.

"They're waiting for me," he said.

Chapter 7

"What're we gonna do?" Ruth Rose asked. "That guy looks mean!"

"Maybe we should just give them the letters," Josh said.

"We can't!" Dink said. "The three sunflower stamps are still in Ruth Rose's house. They'll know we found the stolen stamp!"

"And we can't go home," Ruth Rose said. "They might grab us. Then they'd search us, and they'd find the stamp on Dink."

"Let's cut through the backyards to my house," Josh said. "We can call Officer Fallon and tell him we're being followed!"

"Okay," Dink said. "We can't just stay here."

The kids crawled across Miss Alubicky's lawn on their hands and knees. Suddenly her dog started barking at them.

Dink glanced back at the car. The driver's door flew open. The man in the green suit climbed out of the car and hollered at the kids.

"Let's go!" Josh yelled. They jumped up and raced through Miss Alubicky's backyard.

The man shot after them, crashing through Miss Alubicky's hedge.

"He's coming after us!" Dink cried. "Faster!"

The kids tore across Eagle Lane and

cut into the woods. They hid in some thick bushes to catch their breath.

The man stopped at the edge of the woods. The kids watched as he bent over, catching his breath.

"Come on!" Josh whispered. The minute they started running again, the man plunged into the trees after them.

They were faster than the man. A

minute later, they raced through Josh's yard.

"Run into the barn and climb up to the loft!" Josh yelled.

"But we'll be trapped up there!" Dink said.

"Just do it!" Josh said. "I have an idea!"

The three kids sprinted into the barn. Dink and Ruth Rose scrambled up Josh's rope ladder into the loft.

Below him, Dink watched Josh

shove open the rear door of the barn. But instead of running outside, Josh dove into a pile of hay.

Dink couldn't believe his eyes! "He's staying down there!" he said to Ruth Rose.

"Quick! Get the ladder!" Ruth Rose whispered.

Dink grabbed the ladder and pulled it into the loft.

Seconds later, the man in the green suit barreled through the barn door. Up in the loft, Dink could hear him gasping.

The man looked around the dim barn, then raced out the open rear door.

Dink almost laughed with relief. He started to get up. Suddenly Ruth Rose yanked him back down.

The man ran back into the barn. He stood in the middle and swiveled his head around like a snake.

Dink and Ruth Rose froze and carefully peered over the edge of the loft.

After a minute, the man kicked a pail across the floor and stomped out of the barn.

Dink swallowed and let himself breathe again. He closed his eyes until he heard Josh whisper, "He's gone," from the hay pile.

Dink looked down and saw Josh's head pop up. With hay stuck in his red hair, he looked like a scarecrow.

Dink lowered the rope ladder. He and Ruth Rose climbed down. His legs felt like rubber.

They flopped down in the hay next to Josh. "What should we do?" Dink asked. "That jerk will just go back and sit outside my house."

The kids sat in the cool barn and thought. Then Ruth Rose sat up straight.

"I think I know how we can prove Doris Duncan and O. Bird stole the stamp," she said. "If I'm right, Officer Fallon will arrest them at the same time!"

"How?" Dink and Josh both said.

"I need a telephone," she said. "Can we go in your house, Josh?"

Josh crawled out of the hay and peeked out the barn door. "I don't see anyone," he said.

He quietly opened the door. The kids raced across his backyard and into the kitchen.

"What's your plan?" Dink asked Ruth Rose.

She told him.

Josh threw his arms into the air.

"That is so excellent!" he cried.

Dink's eyes got big, then he grinned. "It's perfect! If it works, the stamp goes back where it belongs and those two crooks go to jail!"

Ruth Rose's first call was to Officer Fallon.

The boys listened as she explained about the letters, the stolen stamp, and her plan.

Ruth Rose listened, then started nodding. "Uh-huh. Got it. Right. Okay, bye!"

"What'd he say?" Dink asked.

Ruth Rose gave Dink a thumbs-up. Then she called information and got the number for the Shangri-la Hotel.

She dialed, then asked, "Is Doris Duncan there, please?"

Ruth Rose grinned at Dink and Josh. She mouthed the words "They just walked in!"

When Ruth Rose started talking,

she used a tough-guy voice.

Dink and Josh listened with their mouths open.

"Hello, Ms. Duncan? My name is Ruth Rose. I'm a friend of Dink's, and I got those letters you want!"

Ruth Rose made a gaggy face at the boys, then continued. "I got yer stamp, too. The one of the upside-down airplane."

She lowered her voice into a deep whisper. "And I know it's worth a lot of dough!"

Ruth Rose listened, then continued. "Dink is so dumb, he didn't know it was valuable. I'll sell it to you for five hundred bucks."

Dink and Josh broke into wide grins. Dink had to stop himself from laughing out loud.

Ruth Rose made a shushing motion with her free hand. "No, not tonight. I gotta go to my grandmother's. I'll meet

you in the library tomorrow at high noon!"

Josh nearly fell on the floor laughing.

"Don't worry," Ruth Rose said. "I'll have the stamp. You just bring the five hundred smackers!"

Then she hung up.

"Ruth Rose!" Josh yelled. "You sounded like a real crook! How did you do it?"

She smiled. "You ain't seen nothin' yet!"

Chapter 8

At noon the next day, Dink and Josh peeked out of Mrs. Mackleroy's office. Ruth Rose was sitting at a table, reading a book.

The library was nearly empty. An old woman sat reading a newspaper. A man was snoozing near the door with his cap pulled over his eyes. Mrs. Mackleroy was on her lunch break.

"Ruth Rose looks so calm," Dink

whispered. "I feel like I'm gonna be sick!"

"If you throw up, I'll kill you, "Josh said. He grinned. "And Mrs. Mackleroy will rip up your library card!"

A minute later, Doris Duncan walked into the library. The man in the green suit followed her. He had long, strong-looking arms and a thick neck.

Dink shuddered. It was the man who had chased them! He nudged Josh as the two walked across the room.

"Are you Ruth Rose?" Dink heard Doris Duncan ask.

Ruth Rose nodded. She held up the five blue envelopes. "The stamp is in here," she said, showing Doris Duncan the empty one.

"I hope Ruth Rose gets the money first, "Josh whispered.

Ruth Rose looked at the man and raised her eyebrows. "Who's he?" she asked in her bad-guy voice.

"This is my associate, "Doris Duncan said. "Mr. Otto Bird."

"Aha!" said Dink in the office.

"Did you bring the cash?" asked Ruth Rose.

The woman snapped her fingers. Otto Bird yanked some bills from his

pocket and handed them to Doris Duncan.

"Lemme see da stamp foist," he croaked.

Josh started to giggle. Dink clapped a hand over his mouth.

Ruth Rose slid the stamp out of the envelope.

"See, there's the upside-down airplane," Dink heard her say.

Otto Bird snatched the stamp out of Ruth Rose's fingers. With his other hand, he whipped out a magnifying glass.

The man examined the stamp through bulging eyes. Then he smirked. "Dis is da one," he said.

Ruth Rose smiled sweetly. "The money, please," she said.

Doris Duncan dropped five one-hundred-dollar bills into Ruth Rose's hand.

In the office, Dink and Josh high-fived.

Ruth Rose counted the money. Out loud. When she finished, she looked at Doris Duncan and Otto Bird.

Then she hollered, "OKAY, OFFI-CER FALLON!"

The man snoozing by the door stood up.

"Don't move, you two!" Officer Fallon said. "You're under arrest for theft and mail fraud!"

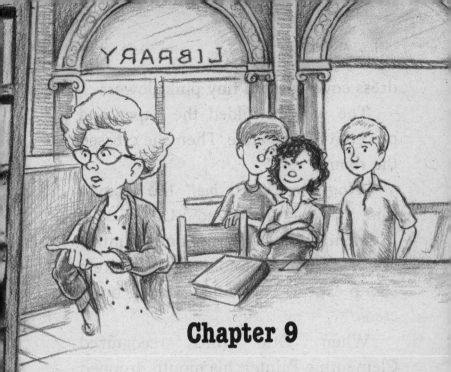

Chapter 9

Officer Fallon snapped handcuffs on the thieves' wrists.

"I'll take that," he said, plucking the Jenny stamp from Otto's hand.

Doris Duncan shot Ruth Rose a nasty look. "You tricked us!" she screamed.

The old woman who had been reading a newspaper suddenly stood up. She had white hair and wore a neat dress covered with tiny pink flowers.

The woman folded the paper and placed it on the table. Then she crossed the room.

"No, *you* tricked *me!*" the woman said. She turned to Otto Bird. "Remember me—Clementine Painter? You lied to me. You told me you were a stamp expert, but you're nothing but a *crook!*"

When Otto Bird recognized Clementine Painter, his mouth dropped open. Not a word came out.

In the office, Dink and Josh danced around Mrs. Mackleroy's desk. "Gotcha!" Dink shouted.

The day before, when Ruth Rose had telephoned Officer Fallon, he told her he'd call Clementine Painter. With her there, Officer Fallon had explained, Doris Duncan and Otto Bird wouldn't stand a chance.

Clementine had hopped on a bus for Green Lawn to get her stamp back.

When Dink and Josh walked out of the office, Doris Duncan's squinty eyes got big. Then they closed, as if she had a bad headache.

Otto Bird's face turned as purple as his tie. Dink thought the man would explode.

"You can't prove nothin'!" Otto Bird yelled. He raised his cuffed hands and pointed at Doris. "She planned the whole thi—"

"Shut up, frog-face!" Doris Duncan snapped at Otto Bird. "If you'd copied down the right zip code, we wouldn't be in this two-bit town to begin with!"

Office Fallon chuckled. "Don't worry, you won't be in two-bit Green Lawn for long. I hear New York has a million-dollar jail!"

Officer Fallon led the stamp thieves

to the door. "I'll meet you folks at Ellie's Diner in an hour," he said over his shoulder.

The kids and Clementine hurried to the window. They saw Officer Fallon lead the two thieves across the street and into the police station.

"My soul," Clementine said to the kids. "That was so exciting. Better than television!"

An hour later, they all met inside Ellie's Diner. Clementine treated the kids to ice cream.

"It feels lovely to be able to buy things for people," she said. "I thought I'd lost that stamp forever."

"How did it get in your vacuum cleaner?" asked Dink.

Clementine smiled, but it was a sad smile. "My mother died recently. She was ninety-six. I was cleaning out her

old vacuum cleaner when I found the stamp. She must have vacuumed it up, but who knows when or where?"

"How did you know it was valuable?" Ruth Rose asked.

"I didn't!" Clementine said. "But I knew it was old, so I looked up a stamp organization in the phone book." She shook her head. "And that's when all the trouble started!"

Officer Fallon nodded. "Otto sang like a bird," he said. "Seems he worked for the stamp outfit you called. When you telephoned to ask about your stamp, he answered the phone."

"He was ever so polite," Clementine said. "He told me to hide the stamp, and he'd come right over to look at it."

Clementine looked angry. "He asked to see the stamp. Like an old fool, I showed him my hiding place."

"Where?" Josh asked.

Clementine blushed. "In my cookie jar," she said. "I treat myself to one cookie every day with my tea!"

Dink laughed. "That stamp has been everywhere!"

"I don't understand how it got under those other stamps," Clementine said.

"Otto Bird hid it under regular stamps so he could mail it to Doris Duncan's home in Colorado," Officer Fallon explained. "They planned to sell the stamp, then split the fifty thousand dollars."

"But why did Otto Bird write those letters?" Dink asked.

"They both have records with the police," Officer Fallon said. "In case anyone opened the envelopes, they had to look innocent. That's why he signed them 'Mother.'"

"And when Doris Duncan got the

notes, she'd know where to find the stamp," Ruth Rose said.

"But she didn't get them!" Josh said.

Officer Fallon smiled. "Right. Lucky for Miss Painter, Otto broke his glasses and copied down the zip code for Green Lawn, Connecticut, instead of Green Lawn, Colorado."

"And then my little brother hid the envelopes in the refrigerator!" Ruth Rose added.

"Mercy!" Clementine said. "All this commotion over a tiny piece of paper!"

Officer Fallon slid an envelope across the table. "Here's your stamp, Miss Painter." He grinned. "Can you find a safer hiding place?"

"You bet, sir!" she said. "This is going right into the bank!"

Everyone said good-bye, and Officer Fallon took Clementine back to the bus station.

The kids walked home, talking about finding a fortune in a vacuum cleaner.

"Want to come over and play more volleyball?" Dink asked.

"Sure. Nate and I were winning!" Ruth Rose said.

Josh grinned. "Not me. I'm going right home. I want to see what's inside my mom's vacuum cleaner!"

Discover the Adventurous and Addictive A-List!

All New!

If you enjoyed this book, check out the other books in the A-List series.

- ☐ The Spy Who Barked #1
- ☐ London Calling #2
- ☐ Swimming with Sharks #3
- ☐ Operation Spy School #4
- ☐ Moose Master # 5

A to Z Mysteries

- ☐ The Absent Author
- ☐ The Bald Bandit
- ☐ The Canary Caper
- ☐ The Deadly Dungeon
- ☐ The Empty Envelope
- ☐ The Falcon's Feathers
- ☐ The Goose's Gold
- ☐ The Haunted Hotel
- ☐ The Invisible Island
- ☐ The Jaguar's Jewel
- ☐ The Kidnapped King
- ☐ The Lucky Lottery
- ☐ The Missing Mummy
- ☐ The Ninth Nugget
- ☐ The Orange Outlaw
- ☐ The Panda Puzzle
- ☐ The Quicksand Question
- ☐ The Runaway Racehorse
- ☐ The School Skeleton
- ☐ The Talking T. Rex
- ☐ The Unwilling Umpire

ANDREW LOST

- ☐ Andrew Lost on the Dog #1
- ☐ Andrew Lost in the Bathroom #2
- ☐ Andrew Lost in the Kitchen #3
- ☐ Andrew Lost in the Garden #4
- ☐ Andrew Lost Under Water #5
- ☐ Andrew Lost in the Whale #6
- ☐ Andrew Lost on the Reef # 7

Available wherever books are sold.
www.randomhouse.com/kids

RANDOM HOUSE CHILDREN'S BOOKS

Z

Was Just the Beginning...

Dink, Josh, and Ruth Rose are off to a camp for detectives! The camp directors have planned a week of mysteries for the campers to solve. But while following the clues, the kids stumble upon a real crime!

Super Edition 1 All new!

AVAILABLE WHEREVER BOOKS ARE SOLD.

   www.randomhouse.com/kids

A to Z Mysteries™

The Absent Author

Dink's favorite mystery writer, Wallis Wallace, has been kidnapped. It's up to Dink and his two best friends, Josh and Ruth Rose, to find Wallis—before it's too late!

The Bald Bandit

A bandit has robbed the Green Lawn Savings Bank! But some kid videotaped the crime. Dink and his friends must find that kid—and his tape—before the bandit does!

The Canary Caper

Pets around Green Lawn are mysteriously disappearing. Dink, Josh, and Ruth Rose won't stop until they track down the thief and return the stolen pets to their rightful owners!

The Deadly Dungeon

Dink, Josh, and Ruth Rose investigate strange noises in Wallis Wallace's castle—only to find a dangerous secret!

A to Z Mysteries™

Join Dink, Josh, and Ruth Rose on all their exciting adventures!

Available wherever books are sold...OR
You can send in this coupon (with a check or money order)
and have the books mailed directly to you!

❑ **The Absent Author** (0-679-88168-9) .... $ 3.99
❑ **The Bald Bandit** (0-679-88449-1) .... $ 3.99
❑ **The Canary Caper** (0-679-88593-5) .... $ 3.99
❑ **The Deadly Dungeon** (0-679-88755-5) .... $ 3.99

Subtotal	$ _____
Shipping and handling	$ 3.00
Sales tax (where applicable)	_____
Total amount enclosed	$ _____

Name _____

Address _____

City _____ State _____ Zip _____

Prices and numbers are subject to change without notice. Valid in U.S. only.
All orders subject to availability. Please allow 4 to 6 weeks for delivery.

Make your check or money order (no cash or C.O.D.s)
payable to: Random House, Inc., and mail to:

A to Z Mysteries Mail Sales, 400 Hahn Road,
Westminster, MD 21157

● ●

Need your books even faster? Call toll-free 1-800-793-2665
to order by phone and use your major credit card.
Please mention your interest code 8703B to expedite your order.

Collect clues with Dink, Josh, and Ruth Rose
in their next exciting adventure,

THE FALCON'S FEATHERS

Josh looked through his binoculars at the other tree.

"That's weird," he said.

"What's weird?" Ruth Rose asked.

"The nest is empty," Josh said.

"Let me see." Dink took the glasses and squinted through the eyeholes.

From his perch, Dink could see directly into the falcon nest. It was woven of twigs, pine needles, and bits of dead leaves. Dink could even see a few feathers. But there weren't any falcons.

Dink looked at Josh with raised eyebrows.

"Where are they?" he asked.

"What's going on?" Ruth Rose asked.

"The baby falcons are gone," Josh told her.